Who MADE My Cheese?

A Parable About Persistent Production

Dave Arnott, Ph.D.

Writers Club Press
San Jose New York Lincoln Shanghai

Who MADE My Cheese?
A Parable About Persistent Production

All Rights Reserved © 2002 by Dave Arnott, Ph.D

Writers Club Press
an imprint of iUniverse, Inc.

For information address:
iUniverse, Inc.
5220 S. 16th St., Suite 200
Lincoln, NE 68512
www.iuniverse.com

This is a work of fiction. All events, locations, institutions, themes, persons, characters, and plot are completely fictional. Any resemblance to places or persons, living or deceased, are of the invention of the author.

ISBN: 0-595-22514-4

Printed in the United States of America

This book is dedicated to people who persistently produce.

CONTENTS

PREFACE

Who Moved My Cheese? makes three assumptions:

> You are dumber than a mouse.
> You create value by consuming.
> You should sniff and scurry your way to success.

Who MADE My Cheese? makes the opposite assumptions:

> You are smarter than a mouse.
> You create value by producing.
> You should persistently produce your way to success.

This book has three sections, much like *Who Moved My Cheese?*

The first section is a reunion where we meet five baby-boomers who reflect on their successes and failures. The very obvious conclusion is that success springs from persistent production, while failure is related to sniffing and scurrying.

The second section is a parable in which the heroines are two Jersey milk cows named Pers (for persistence) and Prod (for production). They persistently produce milk. Their counter-part anti-heroines are two Holsteins that sniff and scurry from one wild scheme to another. They don't seem concerned about their lack of persistent production, because they are confident they will sniff and scurry their way to success. In the end, they find they are seriously mistaken.

The final section of this book offers advice about how to persistently produce in an era where everyone seems to be sniffing and scurrying.

This book is very brief because I do not want to interrupt your persistent production.

Dave Arnott, Ph.D.
March 2002

ACKNOWLEDGEMENTS

Thanks to Spencer Johnson for what he left out of *Who Moved My Cheese?* Cheryl Austin at the City of Rockwall, Texas, introduced me to the "cheese" ideas.

My thinking has been changed for the better by my fellow members of the National Speakers Association of North Texas, who constantly remind me to concentrate on abundance, not scarcity. Perhaps the greatest self-understanding I have experienced was from Ron Lee at Waterbrook Press, who pointed out that my writing makes me "an intellectual smart aleck!"

The administration at Dallas Baptist University continues to be a source of support and encouragement. My fellow professors are a great sounding-board for ideas. I should listen to them more often. My best examples come from my wonderfully insightful students at DBU.

The Chamber of Commerce Leadership program has taught me a great deal about the value of persistently producing.

Commendations to the many accountants who continue to attend my AICPA seminars. Accountants are a great example of the success obtained by persistent production.

Sandee Smith is the creative genius behind the graphics and design of this book and every article I have written, speech I have delivered, and seminar I have led. We are "attached at the brain"–except mine works only on the left side and hers works on both.

You will meet my family in this book. I wish you could meet them in person; they are wonderful. Whatever I have persistently produced is credited to the inspiration of my Mom, Ruth Arnott. The world's persistent production decreased when she left us.

Section One

Persistently Producing…or Not!

PERSISTENTLY PRODUCING IN A SYSTEM

I sat with my four siblings on my sister's porch in South Dakota as we wondered together how the popular book *Who Moved My Cheese?* exemplified our individual lives.

We are all baby-boomers heading for retirement, wondering if we are ready. My oldest brother, Gail, had just retired after thirty years in the Air Force and had bought a huge house in an expensive suburb of Seattle. That particular day, he was looking for a drug company to round out his rather fat stock portfolio. He succeeded in earning rank in the Air Force, retiring as a Colonel. But military service is not exactly a recommended route to riches. His family of five has lived a rather simple life, enabling them to save up a rather nice nest egg for retirement.

"How did you save so much money, even though you had a rather modest income in the Air Force?" I asked.

"Persistently producing," he answered. "I produced for the Air Force by delivering the best course instruction at Air War College." That was true.

Gail was universally admired for the instruction he provided the lieu-tenants who attended his leadership classes.

"And I continued to improve myself when the opportunity presented itself." Right again. Gail had earned a Ph.D. in organizational leadership while in the Air Force.

"Isn't it difficult to make full Colonel rank without having been a pilot?" I asked.

"Yes, it is," he answered. "But I produced for thirty years and the Air Force rewarded me."

"How did persistence contribute to your financial well-being?" I asked.

"When others bought their lunch, I brought my lunch. I have never bought a new car. We only took airplane travel to take care of family members, never as a leisure vacation." Gail has a reputation among our family for being frugal.

He persisted in teaching his three boys about saving and investing.

 When I visited his college-age son at an expensive West Coast University recently, he had just received a check from the $20,000-a-year University because his scholarships had exceeded his tuition and room and board expenses.

Persistently producing has resulted in financial rewards for Gail and his family.

PERSISTENTLY PRODUCING IN INVESTMENTS

Our next brother, Neil, also spent many years in the Air Force and now works for a defense contractor.
He has a glorious house on a bayou in Ft. Walton Beach, Florida, with a ski boat and jet skis in the backyard. He takes his boys snow skiing in Canada each winter. He is able to afford these luxuries even though his wife did not work until recently, and he has never reached a high-level position with his company.

I knew that Neil had been a successful investor over the years. "You must have done a lot of sniffing and scurrying to find the right stocks," I asked.

"No," Neil answered. "My stock picking success can be attributed to a simple concept. I look for companies that persist at what they are doing and produce. Oh, sure, the company will make some incremental changes to what they do. They might change the inputs or the operations or the distribution, but they keep making the same product or service; they just find a better way to make or deliver it."

"But don't you sniff and scurry around trading stocks on a regular basis?" I asked.

"No," Neil answered. "I check on the status of my investments every  day, but I only buy and sell a few times a year. The key to successful investments is to persist with companies who are producing value for their customers."

"Look," he continued, "Everyone knows the status of the markets today. But the future is unknown. I invest in companies that I believe will deliver increased value in the future, not today. Very few successful companies explode out of nowhere and take over a market. If you watch a particular industry long enough, you will see that what seems to be a lightning strike of success is really a persistent plan to produce value for customers."

Neil concluded, "Winning stocks belong to companies who persistently produce value. Winning stock buyers persist with companies who produce."

PERSISTENTLY PRODUCING IN HOBBIES

Our next sibling is Ardell, who has spent 20 years as a nurse at a hospital in Sioux Falls. She has continually turned down promotions to management level positions, because she likes hands-on nursing, and she is good at it. Her husband, Larry, works at the grain elevator in our little hometown of Valley Springs, South Dakota. Yet, on two moderate incomes, they are able to live in the biggest house in town because they have put years of sweat equity into totally refurbishing the three-story, 100 year-old mansion. Larry is one of the most talented and capable guys I know. He can build and repair almost anything. He builds hot rod cars as a hobby.

"Restoring a big, old house and building hot rod show cars must take a lot of sniffing and scurrying around," I asked.

"No," he answered, "If you want to complete a job of that size and complexity, you have to persist and produce."

"I work with farmers, so I know the value of production. When I was a kid, production of 70 bushels of corn per acre was admirable. Now the measure of success is around 150."

"So the most successful farmers are those who sniff and scurry into other industries?" I asked.

"No," Larry answered emphatically. "There are two cash crops in this region," he lectured, "corn and soybeans. The most successful producers adopt a regular rotation between the two. Over the years they have changed fertilizers and pesticides, and now the most sophisticated pieces of machinery have Global Positioning Systems that measure the production in small increments of the field. But they are still farming. And those who persistently produce are making lots of money."

PERSISTENTLY PRODUCING IN PROVIDING CARE

"How had *Who Moved My Cheese?* become such a runaway best seller?" I wondered. Hoping I would find evidence *somewhere* in my family, I turned to my next brother, Dean. He has had two careers: a critical care nurse and a family counselor. He has a wonderful, rambling two-story house in a Norman Rockwell-style neighborhood of Owatonna, Minnesota.

Dean has changed jobs many times, working for various hospitals before obtaining a counseling degree at a Baptist seminary. Since then, he has worked for numerous counseling centers and medical facilities. Certainly sniffing and scurrying had paid off for him, I thought.

"No," he answered. "I have changed jobs a few times, but my career has actually been very strategic. I have always cared for people's needs." He was right; he had not sniffed and scurried. He had put together a wonderful life of caring for the physical, mental, and spiritual needs of others. What seemed like sniffing and scurrying was actually persistent production.

"Caring for people's needs produces the greatest value for them," Dean said. "Humans will always have needs, you might even say that their *needs* persist. As long as I persist in caring for their needs, I will produce value for which I will be rewarded. Oh sure, I have moved from physical to emotional to spiritual needs, but they are all needs. I have persisted in learning about how to care for the whole person. Having been educated and trained in all three: physical, emotional, and spiritual, I am now a practitioner who produces more value than a provider who concentrates on only one element of the human."

"But how can you afford to raise three kids in a nice house with two cars and a motorcycle, while your non-working wife takes trips to London? All on your rather average salary?" I asked. "You must do a lot of sniffing and scurrying."

"Have you read *The Millionaire Next Door*?" he responded. As a college professor and public speaker, there are a lot of books that I quote but have not read cover to cover, and *The Millionaire Next Door* is one of them. The message is that millionaires are common people with common incomes.

"Financial success is not determined by how *much* you make," Dean said, "It is how *little* you spend. I have a comfortable lifestyle with lots of time off to spend with my family because I have persistently produced, I have *never* sniffed and scurried," he said, rather offended that I had accused him of mouse-like activity.

ONE WHO HAS *NOT* PERSISTENTLY PRODUCED

I am next, and last, in my family. I have had six jobs in three distinctly different industries. I have done the most sniffing and scurrying in my family, and I have had the least financial success.

My first job out of college was working for the Association of Tennis Professionals. After five years in pro tennis, it looked like a restructuring of the industry would rob the economic and political power from our organization, so most of us left the ATP in 1981. In 1983, Hamilton Jordan became the Executive Director and led the ATP to a new level of prominence and success that none of us had predicted. If I had persisted  just a few years with the ATP, I would have become a vice president managing a large part of a growing worldwide entity. I should have persisted.

I went from pro tennis to the sports drink business. I worked for Pripps, a Swedish beverage company whose objective was to replace Gatorade as the drink of choice for the athletic crowd. We didn't. When Pripps closed the U.S. operation in 1986, I thought about buying the U.S. distribution rights, but decided it was time to scurry to another industry. Four years later, Coke and Pepsi introduced their own sport drinks, and

anyone with experience in the industry could name their price with these two hugely successful global companies. I was sniffing elsewhere when I should have persisted in the sports drink business.

I used the severance pay from Pripps to buy a small, run-down sporting goods manufacturing company. I turned it around in two years and resold it, just as the sporting goods industry and the U.S. economy were entering the longest sustained growth period in history. I should have persisted.

Next, I put my sports marketing experience to work selling sponsorships for an auto-promotions company. I left after only a year. The sports promotions industry has enjoyed double-digit growth every year since I left. I should have persisted.

Then I entered a project that really demanded persistence. I sought a Ph.D. at the University of Texas at Arlington. Persistence paid off when I earned the degree and became a professor at Dallas Baptist University.

Since learning the value of persistence, I have had some successes. I have completed six marathons, rode my bicycle across the United States, earned a Ph.D., and published a popular book. I am just about done raising two good kids, and I am gaining a reputation as an author, seminar leader, and

public speaker. All my successes can be attributed to persistently producing. All my failures can be attributed to sniffing and scurrying.

My family of five could find no benefit in sniffing and scurrying, but a lot of benefit in persistently producing. Together, we found three problems with *Who Moved My Cheese?* First, we were insulted that the book portrayed the humans, "hem" and "haw" as dumber than the mice. Second, no one creates value by consuming, as the mice "Sniff" and "Scurry" do in the book. Value is created by producing. Third, successful people do not sniff and scurry, they persist.

It was rather obvious that of the five siblings in my generation, the most successful had persistently produced, not sniffed and scurried as the heroic mice in *Who Moved My Cheese?*

At that point, Gail told us the following story about persistent production.

Section Two

The Early Bird May Get the Worm, But the Second Mouse Often Gets the Cheese: A Supply-Side Story About Creating Value

SUNDAY #1: A LESSON ABOUT RISK AND RETURN

"When I was five years old," Gail began, "I was cutting a piece of cheese from a large cheese wheel at our home in Wessington Springs, South Dakota. Like most inquisitive kids, I asked Dad, 'Who made my cheese?'" He said that cheese came from milk, and milk came from cows. If I wanted to know more about it, I should visit the dairy farm that was attached to Wessington Springs Academy, just down the road. The only day I could visit the barn during milking time was on Sunday, so I had to wait until the next Sunday to make my visit.

That Sunday after church, and a big traditional Sunday dinner, I hopped and skipped along the two blocks of uneven sidewalks playing "step on a crack, break your mother's back" until I reached the bottom of dairy hill. I turned up the gravel driveway that angled up to the picturesque white barn nestled into the first knoll of the rambling range of hills that guarded our little town.

The gravel crunched loudly under my little feet as I hiked, so I scooted off into the grass as I reached the barn and the surrounding pasture. I didn't want anyone to know I was there, nor did I want to disturb the cows, so I silently walked over to the milking parlor and peeked through the open door. Good! No one in sight. I walked a few feet to the next door where the gleaming stainless steel milk separator and cheese churn were housed. No one there, either.

I scampered around the corner of the barn and up the stairs to the hayloft. I felt safe there on the second floor where no one would find me. I nestled into the hay at the edge of the hayloft with my eyes just over the open space where hay was thrown into the feeding troughs. From this perch, I looked down into the milking parlor and no one could see me.

I lay quietly in the hay for a few minutes, then one by one the cows meandered through the open door in search of the sweet hay in their troughs. The first two cows were huge, golden brown Jerseys, the champions of milk production. The last two cows were Holsteins, usually associated with milk cows. The only sound was the switching of their tails and the munching of hay, which I could barely hear over the sound of my own breathing.

The smell of fresh hay and ripe cows wafted up through the feeding space, into my nose. I lay quietly watching these massive beasts. I thought I must have fallen asleep and begun to dream, because I thought I could hear one of the Jerseys talking! I turned my head to give my ear the place that my eyes had occupied over the feeding trough. I was right! The Jersey was talking!

From the faint sounds, I figured out that the Jerseys were named Pers and Prod and the Holsteins were named Hop and Jump.

"Where you ladies been all day?" I heard Prod ask Hop and Jump.

"There is a golden grain that grows about ten miles west of here," insisted Hop.

"If we can just walk far enough to get to it, we can eat the golden grain and our milk production will double," added Jump.

"Where did you hear about this golden grain?" asked Prod.

"From an old bull who used to live at the farm south of town," answered Hop.

"Aren't you ladies a little too old and wise to be listening to bull stories?" asked Pers.

"It is true," pleaded Jump. "There is a golden grain, and if we can just reach it, our milk production will double."

"But if you have to walk ten miles to reach it," said Prod, "you will burn up more energy getting there and back than the extra production you will make in milk."

"We have got to keep looking," responded Hop energetically. "It is out there. Our golden grain is just over the next hill. Jump and I are going to sniff and scurry until we find that pot of gold. When we do, we will be rich and you and Pers will be poor cows," she said to Prod.

Pers and Prod each produced 20 pounds of milk that day, because they had stayed close to the barn and saved their energy. Hop and Jump produced only 16 pounds each because they had burned up so much energy wandering the hills looking for the golden grain. But Hop and Jump were not discouraged. They had confidence that they would more than make up the lost milk production when they found the golden grain.

I waited until the cows had been milked and turned out to pasture, then quietly crept down the stairs and around the barn. As I walked by the open door, I could hear the dairyman muttering about the decrease in production from Hop and Jump as he poured the milk into the separator.

I walked down dairy hill wondering which pair of cows would produce the most milk for cheese: Pers and Prod, who limited their risk for a known return, or Hop and Jump, who took greater risk for an unknown return.

I was so fascinated by the talking cows that I continued to visit the dairy barn every Sunday afternoon that summer, and I got a wonderful education on milk, cheese, and the value of persistent production.

Pers and Prod used their huge tongues to moisten the back of a lick-and-stick poster that they attached to the side of the barn that day:

Ecownomics Rule #1:

Udderstand Risk and Return

Sunday #2: A Lesson About Listening to Cowsultants

The next Sunday when I snuck into the hayloft, Pers and Prod were already being milked when Hop and Jump trotted in totally out-of-breath.

"Where have you ladies been?" asked Prod.

"We've been to a milk production seminar over in Alpena," Hop said excitedly. "We talked to a milk production cowsultant from Omaha who said that if we sleep with these ergonomically designed eyeshades, our production will increase ten percent!"

I peered over the edge of the hayloft floor. To my surprise, Hop and Jump each had eyeshades hanging around their necks. The only thing to which I could compare them were the sleeping masks that Rob and Laura wore on the weekly Dick Van Dyke show. I had never seen anyone in our small town wear them, and they looked rather out-of-place hanging around the necks of Hop and Jump.

"Milk production is determined by rest, not activity," lectured Hop.

"Wearing these eyeshades will help us sleep better and our milk production will increase," added Jump. Hop nudged hers into place as a demonstration, but then accidentally hit her chin on the feeding trough, so she slid them back around her neck.

"How much did the eyeshades cost you?" asked Pers.

"Two days production," chimed in Jump. "And a pound a day for the two-year life of the contract.

"You signed a contract giving up a pound a day for two years?" asked Prod incredulously."

"Yes," answered Hop, "But we will easily make up the extra production when we get trained on the proper use of the eyeshades."

"We have a detailed instruction book," Jump contributed, as she turned her attention to the feed in the trough.

"And what about your lost production today?" inquired Pers. "How are you going to make that up?"

"Investments have to be made," answered Hop. "We will easily make up the deficit over the long haul."

I waited again until the amazing cows were turned out to pasture, then moved quietly to a place above the milk separator. I could hear the dairyman verbally calling out the numbers as he weighed the day's production. Pers and Prod produced their usual quantity of twenty pounds each. Hop and Jump's production was reduced to only 12 pounds each because of the energy they had burned in their roundtrip to Alpena.

Hop and Jump each owed the cowsultant 28 pounds of milk, plus a guarantee of a pound a day for the two-year life of the contract. They were confident they could easily pay back the 28 pounds and the pound per day out of the surplus they would be producing as a result of the wondrous eyeshades.

I climbed out of the loft that Sunday with a better understanding of *Who MADE My Cheese*. It was Pers and Prod. I turned as I reached the bottom of diary hill and saw them mounting another sign on the barn:

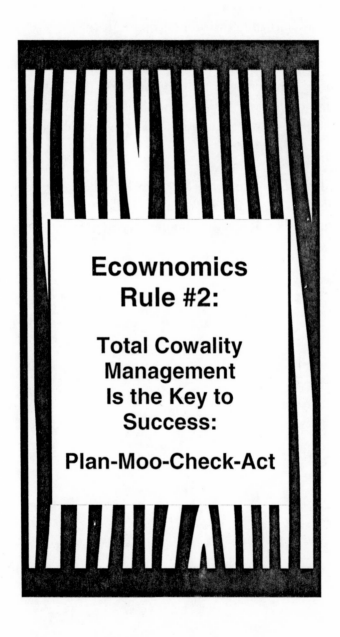

Ecownomics Rule #2:

Total Cowality Management Is the Key to Success:

Plan-Moo-Check-Act

SUNDAY #3: A LESSON ABOUT STAYING AT HOME

The next Sunday I arrived early, anxious to see the success Hop and Jump had experienced as a result of their eyeshades. I was surprised to see only Pers and Prod at the feeding trough. Hop and Jump were nowhere to be found. As Pers and Prod obediently meandered into their stalls, I crept into my listening spot in the hayloft.

Pers and Prod talked about how Hop and Jump had not worn the eyeshades all week. They had sniffed out another get-rich idea that was even better. They got up early and scurried off to Crow Lake for some kind of distribution meeting. As Pers and Prod were being connected to the milking machine, Hop and Jump once again came jogging in the barn in a lather.

"What is that udderly ridiculous sash you are wearing?" Prod asked Hop.

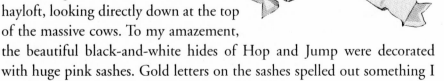

I wiggled to a position where I could see through the floorboards of the hayloft, looking directly down at the top of the massive cows. To my amazement, the beautiful black-and-white hides of Hop and Jump were decorated with huge pink sashes. Gold letters on the sashes spelled out something I could not make out from my vantage point.

"It is not ridiculous," shot back Jump. "These pink ribbons are worn only by associates in the Merry Cow Ash Society."

"And what is that?" questioned Pers.

"It is a moolti-level distribution company," informed Hop. "Jump and I are on the down-line from our sponsor, who gets 10% of our production. We—in turn—sign up down-lines, and we make 10% of all their production. The way we figure it, Jump and I will be driving pink cowdillacs by next spring, while you and Pers will be stuck in this miserable dairy barn for the rest of your lives." Hop and Jump exchanged hoof-high-fives and adjusted their pink sashes as they were hooked up to the milking machine.

"Where are you going to find cows to sign up for this program?" asked Pers. "There are only four of us in this dairy. Half of us are already signed up and the other half don't want any part of it. The nearest dairy is 15 miles north of here, and I doubt if they are interested either."

"You Jerseys are all the same," huffed Hop. "You just want to stay here and produce milk all day. You are missing the future of the milk business, which is not production, but distribution. After each of us signs up 100 down-line producers, we can retire to the back pasture!" she said gleefully.

"But there are not 100 cows in the county!" insisted Prod.

"Then we will just have to travel to find them and sign them up," retorted Jump.

They were not concerned that the long trip to Crow Lake reduced their production to eight pounds that day. Their associate status in the Merry Cow Ash Society would enrich them beyond their wildest dreams in just a few months.

I stood by the edge of the open hayloft door as the cows were turned out to pasture that Sunday. The gold letters on the pink sashes were clear from this vantage point. Hop's read, "Cowabunga!" Jump's was particularly appropriate for her; it read, "The Cow Who Jumped Over the Moon."

The dairyman wondered aloud as to what he was going to do about Hop and Jump's decreasing production of milk. I waited until he left so I could look into the milking parlor. There in grease pencil on a marker board was the day's production data:

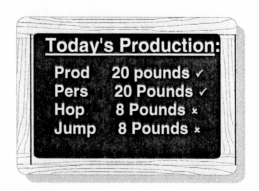

Pers and Prod continued to produce twenty pounds each per day. The long trip to Crow Lake had reduced Hop and Jump's production to only eight pounds each.

I left the barn that day with a better understanding of *Who MADE My Cheese*. It was cows who stay at their post like Pers and Prod. I began to wonder if Hop and Jump were *ever* going to make any cheese!

As I turned from the gravel road onto the broken sidewalk, I stopped for one last gaze at the little white barn on dairy hill. Pers and Prod were mounting a sign that read:

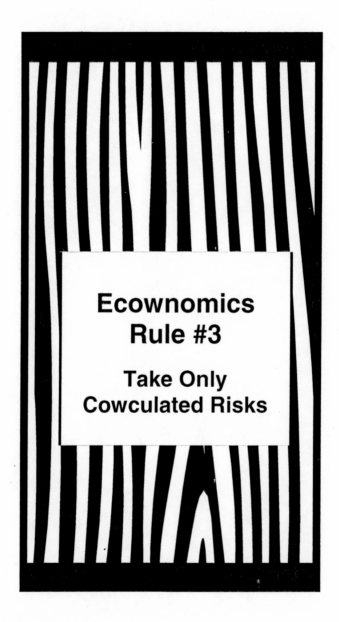

**Ecownomics
Rule #3**

**Take Only
Cowculated Risks**

SUNDAY #4: A LESSON ABOUT DOING WHAT YOU DO WELL

By this time I was accustomed to walking up the dairy hill and finding Pers and Prod happily chewing their cud in the barnyard and Hop and Jump off on some wild excursion. My expectations were met on this Sunday because Pers and Prod were there and Hop and Jump were nowhere to be seen. But I was totally surprised when I crept into the hayloft. Hop and Jump were in their milking stalls—ahead of schedule!

I assumed my customary position in the hayloft and peered over the edge of the worn floorboards. Hop and Jump were harnessed into the strangest looking contraption I had ever seen on a cow! Leather straps around their waists were tied to a machine that reminded me of the weight-reducing shaker that my Aunt Emma used to have in her basement. The belt would shake Aunt Emma and supposedly reduce the flab around her waist. But why would cows want to lose weight?

As I adjusted to look through the floorboards of the hayloft I heard Hop and Jump talking loudly above the roar of the shaking machine.

"This is the best idea we have had yet," shouted Hop to Jump.

"We are going to vertically integrate forward into the milkshake business," Jump announced to Pers and Prod who were now ambling into the barn.

Hop picked up the theme, "We are going to be the first ones to market with a natural milkshake. We are going to shake the milk *before* it leaves the cow, thus cutting out the middle-man who is making all that profit at the Dairy Queen."

"We are going to shake up the milkshake business," crowed Jump, and she and Hop laughed uproariously.

"What did that newfangled machine cost you?" queried Prod.

"Only a week's production," beamed Hop.

"Aren't you concerned that the shaking will remoove some of the fat that is so necessary for good milk production?" asked Pers.

"Oh, we will produce a little less, but profit is so much higher on downstream differentiated goods, that we will easily make up what we loose in production by charging a premium for pre-shaken milk," instructed Jump.

I watched as Hop and Jump unhooked themselves from the machine and staggered into the barnyard. They were both obviously dizzy from the  experience, and maybe even a little sore from all the shaking. Their attitude, however, was like that of a punch-drunk heavyweight boxer, tired but deliriously victorious about moving into the retail milkshake business.

"Pers and Prod, twenty pounds each," called out the dairyman to no one in particular. "Hop and Jump......four pounds each," he sighed. The energy spent running around to buy and install the machine had reduced their production. Also, the shaken milk was harder to extract than regular milk. He picked up the phone and when I heard him talking with the switchboard operator, I thought it was a good time to sneak down the back stairway and out of the barn.

I left that day with a clearer understanding *of Who MADE My Cheese.* Hop and Jump were now making milkshakes, so they made no milk for cheese that day. Now my only hope for eating cheese was based totally on steady cows like Pers and Prod.

I walked backwards down dairy hill so I could get a good look at the sign that Pers and Prod were mounting on the barn:

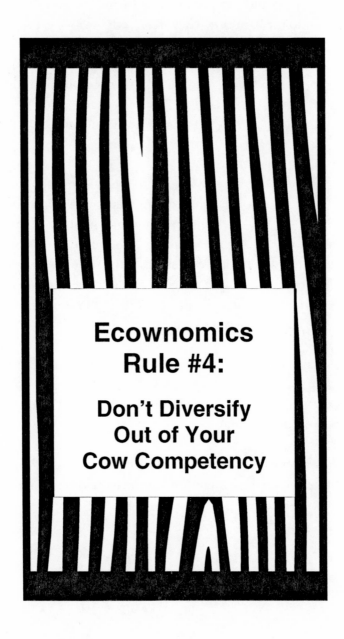

**Ecownomics
Rule #4:**

**Don't Diversify
Out of Your
Cow Competency**

SUNDAY #5: A HARD LESSON ABOUT PRODUCING

I climbed the hill to the familiar sight of Pers and Prod chewing their cud in the barnyard. Apparently, Hop and Jump had scurried off on another wild chase. I crept to my listening post in the hayloft and lay still while Pers and Prod ambled in. I fully expected Hop and Jump to come cruising in with another get-rich scheme, but they did not arrive. Minutes passed with no conversation. Something was wrong. Where were Hop and Jump?

Pers and Prod chewed sweet alfalfa as they were hooked up to the milking machines. Certainly Hop and Jump would appear any minute now with some kind of potion or scientific theory about increased production and plans for wealth beyond their wildest dreams.

But they did not arrive. I began to worry. Sure, Hop and Jump had some wild ideas, but I had grown to enjoy their sniffing and scurrying. Certainly they would come bursting through the door soon with another wild scheme. But they didn't.

Pers and Prod were still silent as I listened for a clue to the whereabouts of Hop and Jump. Finally, Prod broke the silence, "Well, we all know that production and persistence are the keys to survival," she intoned solemnly. Pers did not answer. Prod continued her lecture, "Sniffing and scurrying are exciting, but eventually you have to persistently produce something." Her moralistic tone did not sound good. What had happened to Hop and Jump?

"They should have known…" Prod continued, but her voice was drowned out by the sound of a truck powering its way up dairy hill in first gear. That was strange. The milk truck came on Mondays, not Sundays. I scampered to the edge of the hayloft and peered through the cracks of the barn wall. A truck was backing up to the south side of the barn, but it was not the milk truck. The sign on the side of the truck  read, "John Morrell Meat Packing." I watched in horror as Hop and Jump were herded from a holding pen into the truck.

I walked down dairy hill that day with an answer to my question. Pers and Prod are the ones *Who MADE My Cheese.*

I sadly scuffed my tennis shoes through the gravel tread marks as I descended dairy hill for the last time. As I neared the bottom of the hill, I turned around for one last look. Tears filled my eyes as I read the sign Pers and Prod were mounting on the barn:

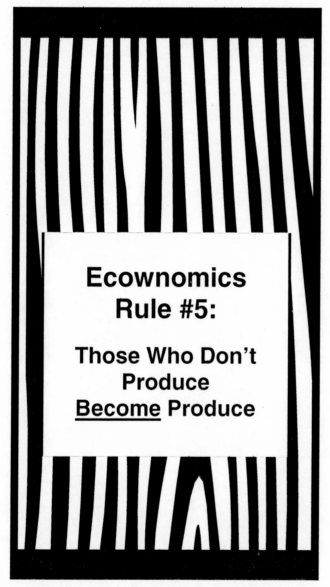

Ecownomics Rule #5:

Those Who Don't Produce <u>Become</u> Produce

Two mice sniffed and scurried under the sign, because Hop and Jump would no longer produce anything for them to consume.

Section Three

The Moral of the Story: Persistently Producing is Better Than Sniffing and Scurrying

PERSISTENT PRODUCTION

It was very quiet around the table as Gail finished the story. Five mature adults were misty-eyed about the death of two mythical talking cows.

Since that afternoon on my sister's porch in South Dakota, I have told that story to dozens of classes, seminars, and association meetings. It is surprising how seemingly battle-hardened corporate executives get so sentimental over the loss of two cows. I think it is because they understand the metaphor, and they are sad at the loss of their workmates and friends who sniff and scurry around until they are fired, go bankrupt, or get competed out of the marketplace.

That is because the only people who hear me tell the story are **persistent producers** who do not sniff and scurry around chasing the latest fad. Those who chase wild ideas are not around to attend my meetings.

I have asked numerous groups for examples of Fortune 500 companies who have succeeded by sniffing and scurrying as advised in the parable *Who Moved My Cheese?* We have yet to find one airline that has sniffed its way into automobile production. There are no steel manufacturers who have scurried their way into the grocery business. No university

has sniffed into building construction, and no church has scurried into the stock brokerage business.

INCREMENTALLY CHANGING THE INPUT

Oh sure, organizations change the input. But they do not go on such wild chases after golden grain that they forget to feed the cows. The steel wheel replaced wooden wheels, but neither wagons nor cars went without wheels during the change-over. Diesel engines replaced steam powered railroad trains, but train service did not stop for months in the meantime. The industry continued to persistently produce through the changes in their means of input.

The Dangers of Corporate Level Sniffing: Know What Business You're In!

Pepsi sniffed and scurried its way into the fast food industry when it bought KFC, Pizza Hut, and Taco Bell. After a few years, they spun the restaurants off into a separate entity called Tricon Global restaurants and "scurried" back into persistently producing soft drinks.

Sears sniffed into a disaster by buying Allstate Insurance and Dean Witter investments. They quickly scurried back to their core retailing business where they persistently produce profits.

The Perils of Core Competency Sniffing: Do What You're Good At!

Michael Jordan is arguably the best basketball player in history. He sniffed over to baseball and scurried back to basketball. Then he sniffed into management with the Washington Wizards and scurried back onto the basketball court. There is a lesson in this for the rest of us: If you want to earn the greatest return from society, do what they pay you the most for. For Michael Jordan, it is playing basketball. When he persistently produces what he is good at, he earns much higher returns than when he sniffs and scurries into what he is bad at.

Shawn Bradley is the 7-foot-6-inch center for the Dallas Mavericks of the NBA. When the team fell on hard times in the late 1990's, Bradley could have looked at empty seats during a Mavericks game, then returned to the same arena the following night to find it sold out for a Stars hockey game. Bradley was wise enough not to sniff into hockey skates! He persistently produced for the Dallas Mavericks. In 2002, there is a new team owner and a new arena packed with fans to watch Bradley play for the now-popular Mavericks. Bradley is glad he did not sniff and scurry. He has been rewarded by persistently producing.

INCREMENTALLY CHANGING OPERATIONS

Successful companies change production technologies, but they do not forget to produce milk while they are making the change. Enron was a highly successful natural gas distribution company that sniffed and scurried its way into the trading of many commodities like electricity and bandwidth. Enron's success in gas trading was not replicated in its other businesses.

In the aftermath of September 11, 2001, the airline industry suffered massive losses. The only airline to declare a profit in the fourth quarter was Southwest Airlines who continued to fly only 737 aircraft and provide only point-to-point travel. They

have refused multiple temptations to sniff and scurry. They keep following the same business model that has persistently produced success for them while other airlines suffer by sniffing and scurrying around.

INCREMENTALLY CHANGING DISTRIBUTION

All organizations should look for new distribution channels that will enhance their performance, but not at the cost of current production.

The town crier was replaced by newspapers, which eventually had competition from radio, then TV and the Internet; but the customer continued to get the same value: Information. The customer simply got it via a

different distribution technology. In Dallas, the Belo Corporation owns the Dallas Morning News, WFAA-TV, a cable news channel, and supplies Internet sites. The company has not sniffed and scurried, they have persistently produced information that travels via changing technologies.

Belo tried to tie their TV broadcasts together with the Internet. They sent an instrument called a "cue-cat" (sort of a computer mouse with a UPC reader) to each household in North Texas. They soon discovered the financial pain associated with sniffing and scurrying too far. The operation was closed after less than a year, and Belo stopped sniffing and scurrying and returned to the persistent production of news. (Editor's note: Thanks to Dr. Arnott for finally passing up the opportunity to play with a creative term: "cat and mouse.")

INCREMENTALLY INVESTING IN THE FUTURE

Companies certainly should invest in the future, but not at the cost of the present. Iridium was praised as a revolutionary way to communicate via a worldwide satellite phone. The phone messages bounced off low-level satellites, so the system was not reliant upon local towers. The idea was so ahead of its time that Iridium went broke, and the satellites were tragically allowed to fall back into the atmosphere. An incremental move from a land-based to a satellite-based system could have been successful. Sniffing and scurrying caused the company's downfall.

Priceline.com was an early-mover success story in the distribution of unsold airline tickets and hotel rooms. Those businesses are related and the venture made good sense. Their sniff and scurry into home mortgages did not succeed, and they were soon sent scurrying back to persistent production of airline tickets and hotel rooms.

Producing is Better Than Consuming

I have asked groups for examples of individuals or companies that have been enriched by consuming, like "Sniff" and "Scurry" in *Who Moved My Cheese?* Those characters spend their lives consuming cheese. I have not found one case where anyone has experienced long-term enrichment by consuming. But my audiences have a plethora of stories about individuals and companies who have been enriched by **producing** goods and services that create value for consumers

In economic terms, you enrich yourself by trading what you have for what you do not have. That is because, in a competitive market, it is a good assumption that the arms-length trade was to your benefit. However, after buying (eating cheese) for a while, you have to take a break and sell your services or labor (produce some milk) or you will quickly spend yourself broke!

In your personal and your business life, you will find many examples of the fallacy of sniffing and scurrying and many examples of the success produced by **persistently producing**. Do not sniff and scurry. Persistently produce.

Section Four

Workbook

ECOWNOMICS RULE #1:

UDDERSTAND RISK AND RETURN

When have you sniffed and scurried after the equivalent of "golden grain" when you should have continued to persistently produce?

Ecownomics Rule #2:

Total Cowality Management is the Key to Success:
Plan—Moo—Check—Act

Cite an example of when you have listened to cowsultants when you should have followed your own instincts.

ECOWNOMICS RULE #3:

TAKE ONLY COWCULATED RISKS

When have you chased unwise distribution schemes at the expense of persistent production?

ECOWNOMICS RULE #4:

DON'T DIVERSITY OUT OF YOUR COW COMPETENCY

When have you tried something outside of your competency base that reduced your persistent level of production?

ECOWNOMICS RULE #5:

THOSE WHO DON'T PRODUCE **BECOME** PRODUCE

Throughout your career, what examples have you seen of individuals or organizations that failed to produce and lost their career or business?

EPILOGUE

If the original *Who Moved My Cheese?* was helpful for you, I'm glad. Imitation is the greatest form of flattery, and I trust author Spencer Johnson feels that way about the rejoinder I've written. The great popularity of "cheese" is testimony that we need to be encouraged to change. However, while changing, we must be careful not to change what should remain constant.

Balancing change and stability is a difficult issue. However, it seems like the business book industry is awash with "change" books that continually emphasize the successes of change, while ignoring the dangers. As the third section of this book points out, there are numerous examples of changes that not only failed, but *prevented* the organization from being successful. If the organization had not changed at all, they would have been successful. *Any* change prevented their success. The change is made worse by the fact that they changed to a modus operandi that was even worse than what they were doing. The organization changed out of their purpose for being, or core competency, and thus change prevented success.

Managers are currently enchanted by change agents because change is exciting, while status quo is boring. As *The Millionaire Next Door* indicates, persistent production is the most proven path to success. But it's boring. It's difficult to stand in front of a Board of Trustees or Executive Managers and intone, "We're going to persistently produce the same product in the same manner." It's boring, but it works. As this book points out, there's certainly nothing wrong with making incremental changes in production, operations, marketing, and distribution. But wholesale changes of the "sniffing and scurrying" scale are seldom successful.

In your career, investing, relationships, or any other venture, persistence is the greatest predictor of success. You can certainly think of people who have been successful in any number of ventures, and once you got to know them you were surprised at how a person of seemingly average competency could be so successful. There are always smarter, more competent people who have less than impressive levels of success because they failed to persist. At the same time, those with the greatest level of success are those who persisted.

The careers of successful executives often seem complex, like the description of Dean's career in the opening section of this book. But, when analyzed from a longer view, it becomes clear that changes are a means of persistently producing value for consumers.

A dynamic investment portfolio seems more exciting than one that holds to a consistent strategy. Exciting, but far less successful. A portfolio that sticks to a consistent strategy will experience ups and downs, but in the end will show a greater long-term return than one that continually "sniffs and scurries" among a number of different strategies.

Relationships demand a high level of persistence. If you've been married, you know that persisting through difficult times not only produces a successful relationship, but a more meaningful one. There's even some evidence that relationships that have been through tough times are stronger and more rewarding (more productive) than those that have not. "Sniffing and scurrying" is definitely not good for marriage relationships. If you've had kids, you know that they can give you the most rewarding and most challenging events of your life. Persistence teaches THEM how to persist and builds character in them. A continually changing set of behaviors from a parent is schizophrenic and produces a confused and unruly child.

Who Moved My Cheese? and *Who MADE My Cheese?* present two ends of a continuum about how much or little to change. The combination of the two books will give you a good look at both ends of the scale.

It's my hope that *Who MADE My Cheese?* has provided you with a great appreciation for the value of persistent production.

ABOUT THE AUTHOR

Dave Arnott, Ph.D., is an author, speaker, consultant, seminar leader, and college professor. He is the author of the acclaimed book, *Corporate Cults*, by AMACOM press. The first printing sold out in five weeks and the book was nominated as a business book of the year.

The notoriety of the book has made him one of America's top authorities on the issue of corporate culture, and he has appeared on the CBS program *48 Hours* and a national TV morning show. Dr. Arnott has appeared on numerous TV programs and multiple radio shows. He is quoted regularly about individual-organization relationships in national and local media outlets that include *Fortune* magazine and *Training* magazine. He has authored numerous applied and research articles in leadership, strategy, and international management.

He is an accomplished keynote speaker who dazzles audiences with his voluminous poetry memorization and story-telling ability that relate organizational relationships to very practical situations.

Dr. Arnott has consulted with numerous organizations on the topic of improving strategic goal completion and organizational culture change. He has authored many seminars and personally led over 100 days of seminars on the topics of leadership, management, communications, and team-building.

He is a professor of management at Dallas Baptist University where the students voted him the Professor of the Year in the College of Business.

His Ph.D. is in strategic management from the University of Texas at Arlington. His dissertation was on the topic of U.S.-Russian joint ventures.

Dr. Arnott worked for the Association of Tennis Professionals before entering the consulting and academic fields. He also worked in the sporting goods and sports promotions industry where he was owner/manager of a small manufacturing company and a marketing director.

He lives in the Dallas suburb of Rowlett, Texas, with his two college-age children. He makes frequent visits to his writing retreat in Angel Fire, New Mexico. Dr. Dave is a retired marathoner who once rode his bicycle across the U.S.

More details are available on his website: *www.davearnott.com*

The Dave Arnott Company
3509 Scott Drive
Rowlett, Texas 75088
972.475.7164
dave@davearnott.com